Dedication

I dedicate this book to my nieces and girlfriends experiencing new challenges in their lives that getting older can spring upon you. I pray this book will be the antidote for a smoother transition and hope that sharing my many surprise attacks will benefit many going through the change of life.

Getting Old is Not For Chumps

How to Enjoy Life and Age Well

DEBORAH WELLS

Getting Old Is Not For Chumps: How To Enjoy Life and Age Well
By Deborah Wells

ISBN # 979-8-218-18119-2

Author: Deborah Wells
Editor: Valerie L. McDowell
Cover Design: danny_media
Interior Book Design: Velin@Perseus-Design.com
Publisher: Power2Excel Agency, LLC

Contents

Introduction

Looking back at the many changes I have encountered in this body since I started going through my senior menopausal years, I wondered if anyone else was discovering what I was experiencing. So I thought it would benefit other seniors to be more informed about what to expect. I know some doctors will discuss these symptoms as you go through them, but how many of us would like to be informed before we get there? We are all getting older with each passing year and are blessed to keep breathing in fresh oxygen. If you have reached 55 years and received your senior 10 percent discount card, you have an additional perk for triumphing through life's hard knocks.

Aging is not for the faint of heart. But, as I slip, slide, and bump my way into a body I can hardly recognize at times, or often even want to junk it for parts; I vow not to go down like a chump. And for the rest of you who need a supernatural reason to leave the house after 9:30 pm, let me share some of my adventures in old age and senior years. And by the way, I plan to make the most of it, especially doing some things I put off for far too long.

CHAPTER 1

Spunky Lady

Lying in bed with one eye open and stretching, I want to savor a little more comfy bedtime. I turn to look at the clock and realize what day it is. "Oh my gosh, I'm supposed to walk with a few other women at the park today." We had started a walking club just a few months before this. So, I drag myself out of bed, look out the window, and see the sun beaming down rays of glorious sunshine. That's the best kind of motivation. Quickly, I get myself together and rush up to the park. Everybody is already stretching, and one of our group participants says, "You generally beat us all here. What's up with you this morning?" "Oh, just a lazy bug," I say. "Nothing I can't shake off!" I generally have a lot more energy when I get up, but on this day, I don't know what is weighing on me. I feel like a snail. I have always thought of myself as the rabbit in that race with the tortoise, but you don't always know what a day will bring when you are not used to waking up in an aging body.

There's not too much that I will let get me down—not the pain, not the weather. But this particular day is just a little different. Still, I tell myself this is nothing I can't shake off. Ahh, I realize the sun is doing its job this morning. I love sunshine; it always rejuvenates me, and I need all that vitamin D. So, here I am, jogging in place and bouncing around; suddenly, I am more than ready to take on the day.

Looking back to another run, this one with my younger sisters on a warm summer day, I remember them lagging. I coached them some and teased some more, "Okay, you young ladies, we'll have to pick up the pace if we are going to finish this marathon walk. Let's not take all day." So I got them moving that day.

A few years later, I felt like I was lagging, like the tortoise in the race. The problem was my ankles. My hips or back had gotten a knot in them, restricting me from moving fast and free. I knew I needed to stay active, but my body was fighting me like we were in a contest. When I ran, the pain was trying to get the best of me, but I was determined not to let this new, slow, older body take control of my mind or body. I kept telling myself, "Mind over matter, mind over matter," pressing home the point that I refuse to be the tortoise in any race.

I learned then that walking does a body good, and being in the sunshine and staying in constant motion is uplifting. I'm like a flower—I light up when I feel the sun's rays. I tell myself, "Keep walking, girl, keep walking, walking; walk that pain out!" And that's what happens as you continue to walk. You feel the pains fading away.

Back in the present, pulling those hills and having good conversations at the park made the walk more pleasurable. We even lost track of how far we had walked, but it was all worth it. I think that once you become a certain age, you have more appreciation for people and life. Sometimes, after our walks, we eat a light breakfast to top off the morning. I know how conversation and food can impact our overall mental health, so I try to stay engaged. I have always been one who has spent much time with my young nieces, so I would allow them to come over with my granddaughter for a weekend of fun and activities. We would go bicycling, walk to the park, have a hula hoop contest, and play with water balloons. I would encourage this togetherness about twice a year. Sometimes they would get out of hand a little, but we were just being silly, and I was happy I could always keep up with them.

We did this visiting thing for a few years. I was in my fifties and sixties then, and my body allowed me to hang on. I remember how I used to love to go roller skating. It was a weekly thing for me. However, as I got older and some pain set in in my knees and hips, I realized that if I wanted to keep my health and legs working, I could not continue to roller-skate because my joints did not move nor turn like they used to. But I didn't stop everything just because I couldn't skate. Oh, no! I just traded in that activity for what I could do without strain and started walking more. I also formed a couple of women's book clubs to stay sharp mentally and to encourage others to find stories they loved. Our book club always consisted of six to eight senior women. Reading fiction keeps the mind sharp.

I can still play volleyball, and when family or friends get together, I show them what I am made of. I have strength for all of our outdoor activities. I may have to pay for it later, but I get a burst of energy while in the moment.

When we get together for outdoor activities, I usually bring all the games because I still know what the young people and the seniors like. I can recall a couple of years ago when my granddaughter, who was nine years old, would come to spend the summer with me. And just like any child, she was always restless and inquisitive and wanted to know what we would do each day. But, of course, since I have retired, my days are free to make my schedule and do things I have always loved. Beautiful flowers and gardening are two of them.

I started volunteering at my cousin's garden and farm to quench this love. I go two days a week, two to three hours each day. I happily discovered that this garden site had everything to help me become a better outdoors person and a top-notch gardener.

By becoming a volunteer, I was able to reap many more benefits, such as horticultural classes, aquaponics, and meeting people from all walks of life. That is why once you learn the art of gardening, you gain much knowledge about different types of flowering perennials and annuals and how to create viable garden soil instead of just using dirt. You learn how to prune plants and trim trees and hedges. There is something rejuvenating to me about being out in nature and smelling the fragrances and watching the bees and butterflies. Without any thought, they are busy doing their job to make God's beautiful earth flourish and bring forth new food and new life. There's a time and a season for everything, especially planting and growing.

I got my love for gardening and flowers from my mom and my grandma. My mom grew up in Elberton, Georgia, and farming and picking cotton was their way of life. Grandma loved having beautiful flowers in her front yard and large pots on her porch.

My Mom and Dad moved to Cleveland, Ohio, where I made my home. I can remember, as a teenager, every year going back to Georgia to spend time with my grandma. As my grandma got older, I did much of her planting and learned more about gardening. Sometimes when volunteering at the garden site now, I feel like a rabbit in a cabbage patch. I seem to have all I need for the moment, and the closeness to God and nature does my body and mind good. The fragrance of the air, the flowers, and the wind blowing so gently on my face all seem to have a special relationship with these plants. I can even feel what they're saying. Their telepathic vibes ask me if they can get some of these weeds off my lap. Or they're saying I'm so thirsty; please give me some water. I love to see trees and flowers thrive. I believe they know that I'm their closest and best companion when I'm around them. I make them happy, and they thrive.

Let's get back to my precious little bored granddaughter that needs something to do and places to go. I enjoy cooking and trying new dishes, which most children do not want to do. I think the older generation has much experience to offer the younger generation, and I plan on sharing quite a bit of my knowledge with my grandchildren and others.

As you can probably guess, I told her I have some great things planned for her daily. I always like to get to the garden early in the morning, so I generally get up there around 10 a.m. My Jayda is nothing like I was. She said the sun's too hot, the bugs are scary, and she doesn't want to get dirty. However, I did take her a few times and teach her how to identify and pull weeds, how to pull dead leaves off the flowers, and how to plant new baby flowers. All she liked was watering the flowers. I promised her we would go for ice cream when we finished. I can easily spend 2 to 3 hours in the garden and get lost in nature. But every good thing must come to an end.

We drove home, put the car in the garage, rested, and had a sandwich for lunch. About an hour later, I asked Jayda if she was ready to go and get some ice cream. "Yes, Yes," she replied and ran, jumping into the car. I told her that we were going to walk. We need to exercise our legs a bit more. She replied, "I'm still tired from the garden."

I went on to tell her how our arms and legs are two of our body's greatest commodities. Your legs will take you on great adventures every day at home and outside of the house. But I believe in the old saying, you either use them or lose them. Exasperated, Jayda says, "Okay, no more of your stories. Let's go."

While walking, she asked how far the ice cream store was. I replied that it was about 2 miles going and coming back home. "Grandma, don't you ever get tired? Jayda asked. I don't like walking as much as you do, I like to sit in the car, and we can drive sometimes." I said, "Oh, I do too, but don't we want strong muscles for our legs? So we're going to exercise these legs as much as we can, especially when it's nice and warm outside, and that way, you'll appreciate it later." "Yeah, I bet, but I don't," she sighed. After arriving, we sat in Baskin-Robbins for about an hour and savored every spoonful of our delicious sundae.

It was now time to start our hike home. The walk back was shorter because we had revived our energy. I kept those days very active because I didn't want to hear my Jayda say she was bored. I took every opportunity to get some exercise when I had free time. Sometimes it was at the gym, walking, or maybe playing tennis. I did all I could to ensure I didn't let my body get in a slump with too much inactivity.

This new generation loves to watch movies and do a lot of computer time, which is okay, but it's motionless. This body will give us good service well into our 80s and 90s if we learn to take care of it.

I intend to lend you insight into how to accomplish this if you will only take heed. For those of you that say you want to do better, you can. Just remember it's mind over matter. You may start off stiff with a few aches and pains here and there, but you must train your mind to want to do better and sometimes tell yourself "Yes, I'm older, but a few pains do not matter." This is the only way to regain your health and strength.

I have seen so many of my family and friends turn into such old-acting people too soon because of a few pains. Don't let the couch, bed, and television become your constant companions. Get that spunk back in your mind first, then make your body conform to your thoughts. Children will eagerly help you out and make you want to do more. I plan on being the rabbit in this race of life and not just tugging on like a tortoise. Life's too short, and it's meant to be enjoyed. Jesus said, *"I came that you might have life and that more abundantly."* John 10:10.

Stay active, pray, see your doctor regularly, and let's get on with this race of life.

CHAPTER 2

Exercise and the Gym

Deborah on her stationary bike.

I can remember how much exercise I got every day when I was working. I got up early every morning, about 6 a.m. I gave myself an hour to do all I had to do to get my day started before running out the door. I was headed to my good government job, which began at 7:30 a.m. The parking lot of our job facility was quite a distance from the building. My walk from the parking lot to my building and then to my office was about a quarter of a mile. That hike got me ready for whatever came my way in the form of walking; my legs were ready.

I would generally walk around the building three days a week for about a mile during my lunchtime. I also formed a walking club with six other health-conscious people during this time. We would meet at different Metro parks every other Saturday morning and take a 3-to-4-mile hike around the hiking trail. We all had the same agenda: maintaining our independence long into our golden years. I have never liked lying around watching a lot of television. That's why meeting at the park at 9 a.m. was easy and not a problem for the group, especially when we enjoyed the warm sunshine and fresh air. These actions were a recipe for good company and all worthwhile. It helped us put some pep in our steps, enthusiasm In our minds, and energy in our bodies.

During our Saturday walks at the park, we generally start with stretching, a few twists, and a little jogging in place, and then we go off. I will walk gently, starting on a flat surface as we walk. The walking trail picks up a little incline after about half a mile. That hill puts a little pull in the calf of our legs. After about another half mile, the trail levels back out onto flat ground. The walk is very invigorating. It makes us feel like we have been through an obstacle course. We do this 3-4 mile walk every other Saturday, and I think all participants really look forward to this outing. I know I do, even though my joints may ache. I am proud that my legs can push and walk quite a distance once I start. To anyone with aches and pains, this is a great way to help push through the pain and give you more flexibility in your joints. Now, I only walk occasionally, but I also have a treadmill and hand weights at home.

My routine as a non-working person has shifted a bit. I no longer get up at 6 a.m. Since retiring, I have taken those couple extra hours to stretch and to watch The Daily News. But I am in no way a bed bug, a person that loves lying around. I still start my day early, only now I sleep until about 8 or 8:30 in the morning. However, my morning routine is a little different now. I get some exercises done in bed before I swing my legs over to the side and sit up.

Every morning I lie flat on my back, and I pull my head up to my chest as far as I can until I can feel the pull in my stomach muscles; I do this in sets of ten for about twenty seconds for each sit-up. After this, I sit on the side of the bed and pick up my little hand squeezer made of heavy rubber that my daughter gave me for my 70th birthday. She told me this would keep my hands and fingers strong if I used it daily. It is a little pink rubber circle with the center of it open. I take it in one hand and squeeze it as hard as possible until the hole in the center is closed. The sturdy rubber makes it very hard to close, but I do it every morning before going into the bathroom. There was a time about two years before this when I was having a problem squeezing out my washcloth, but not anymore. I have strong hands now because I am determined to be independent and consistent with my exercise and workouts.

After getting dressed for the day, I generally get my two 5-lb. weights that I use every other day, lifting them over my head up to my shoulders and swinging them around my waist 20 times each. There are so many ways to exercise, but you can do more and more as you age to keep your body in motion and flexible.

Another way I incorporate exercise is through travel. I come from a relatively large family, and most of our family did not travel much. But I formed a vacation club for our children when they were young. After that, I did vacation planning for the whole family. I would research the most family-friendly places I could find so we could get out and enjoy other cities and attractions. Traveling and sightseeing are great forms of exercise. I have heard many of my family and friends say that as they age and their legs get harder to use, they want to live in an apartment where all the rooms are on one floor. I used to think like that too, but not anymore. As you age, you should continue to live and learn. All the people I know who traded their homes with steps for one-level living in apartments have unknowingly cheated themselves out of exercise for their legs and back.

One-level living may be comfortable, but it is not challenging. I am not saying this is better for sick or disabled people. I am only speaking for seniors with a strong mind to continue moving about for a healthier lifestyle. Besides, I am speaking from experience. All the time, while I was walking with a cane, my ankles, legs, and back, were in constant pain. But I continued walking those 14 stairs in my home at least twice daily. It was a press and painful, but I pushed myself to continue. My grown son used to tell me when he was my trainer at the gym not to be a wimp and remember that if there is no pain, there is no gain. So I started lifting 20-lb. weights on the curl machine, and through regular persistence, I can now lift 40-lbs.

Leg lifts were great in strengthening my calf and thigh muscles. I did several other machines according to how I was feeling that day. I try to go to the gym at least twice a week. However, I know that sitting too long daily can cause my joints to stiffen. I remember watching my mom battle diabetes, cancer, and other debilitating ailments as she pushed herself every day until she could no longer because of a stroke. She did all she could while she had the strength to do it.

I do not have any of the sicknesses that my mother had. I am only going through painful arthritis, so I will keep this body in motion and exercise as much as possible. I know I need to exercise more; that's why I joined Planet Fitness so that even when the weather is dreary and I can't work in my garden, I can still get my workout. Although some days, I admit I have to talk to and encourage myself to get to the gym. It is a struggle sometimes to get to a mind-over-emotions decision, and often, anything that will help the body, the mind will fight against it. I still get exercise at home, but it's not enough. It is so easy once you get older to tell yourself, "Oh, this is my time, and I'm going to relax; cook me a good meal or go out to dinner; come back home, watch a good movie." Don't get me wrong, I do all of this too, and I think it's great, but do not slip into a life of ease and become too complacent at the expense of your health.

I plan to incorporate a healthy lifestyle into my day-to-day living. As we age, we really cannot become lazy; it will only cause our hearts to weaken, and our energy level will be zapped from you. Remember the cell phone and the television, and the computer. They're all great to use, but they are a time robber. I always love to get out and meet new people. I have never met a stranger; I can talk with anyone. That is actually how you meet new people. I like to try new challenges. Most every community has programs for seniors. I joined a yoga class; maybe you have joined up with Zumba or a dance class, but whatever class or exercise you're comfortable with, I say try it out. You never know if an activity will be a fit until you try it. Don't be a wimp.

You can do many leisure activities to maximize your golden years. Some are outreach programs specifically targeted to seniors, but these activities and challenges often start while you are still relatively young and working, like in your fifties and sixties. So don't just talk about how you want to stay active throughout your senior years, do it even if you have to make some lifestyle changes because it is well worth it.

I found that the gym was the right fit for me. I could not work out on all of the machines, but I did the ones I could do every week. I started only able to lift a few weights on the leg lifts and sometimes the elliptical. I started on the elliptical doing 2-3 minutes, and I gradually was able to stay on it for 10 and 15 minutes. Anything that you can't do, progressively do what you can until your strength and endurance come. I started on the weight machine and gradually increased the weight over time. I can see that it is making a difference in my muscle strength and arm strength.

Whenever I go to the gym, I still have to talk myself into getting up and telling myself I need this. It's as if I'm talking to someone else, "Come on, come on, you can do this." So I get up and press on. I say to anyone, do not allow yourself to lie in bed the entire morning and only get up when you are hungry to get something to eat or go to the doctor. Tell yourself every day, will you try to do a new challenge? If you don't have a husband or wife, that's okay. What about a family member or good friend? You may even say that since I've become older, I have lost many family members and never had many friends. Well, I will tell you, like my mom always told me, if you want friends, you have to show yourself friendly. And don't get mad at every little thing people say or do. We can obtain friends at any age.

This attitude has helped me to have a core group of friends in my circle. It's always good to have someone like-minded that can encourage you regardless of what's going on in your life. I find that many older people have allowed the struggles of life to beat them down, and it has caused them to become withdrawn from some things and people that can help them. Did you know that walking around the shopping mall is a form of exercise, and you're getting out and meeting people? I do it when it is cold and dreary outside. I don't feel like going to the gym, but I know I need to exercise, so I'll go to the shopping mall. I'll window shop and maybe have lunch or a bite to eat after exercising. The more you get out and walk, the better those joints will feel. But again, I'm speaking from experience. I refuse to spend my days just sitting around the house on the computer, watching TV, or talking on the telephone, although I stay in touch with family and friends.

Walking and a proper diet will give you a new outlook on life. We will discuss good eating and diet in more detail later in the book. Trust me; diet is everything. I can say that everything you do in this body starts first in your mind. If you feed your mind with knowledge about world events, foods, exercise, and God, you can do great things in this life and your senior years. Trying to help someone who needs a little encouragement will also help you and encourage you to keep pushing forward. My daughter works with seniors at the YMCA, and she always tells me how so many of them do swimming, weightlifting, bicycling, and much more.

I am encouraged to hear that they have chosen a healthy lifestyle. I used to love to go bike riding. I have a nice 10-speed bike in my garage that I have not ridden in over 15 years because of the limited mobility in my hip joints. That is the only limitation that I have because of my arthritic joints. This is why I walk so much and go to the gym. I know it helps to strengthen my legs, and it will also help alleviate the pain when they try to get stiff. Every excuse that my mind tries to tell me that my body can't do, I push past it, and I tell myself that this too shall pass, and I press on.

I am still looking forward to one day riding my bike again. Summertime is an excellent time to find outside activities. Don't just be that person who likes to sit in the window and watch life and the birds as they pass you by. Gardening is an excellent activity for anyone of any age to take up. Even if you cannot get down into the dirt, you can you can grow flowers in windowsill pots. Or you can volunteer at a garden place. It will cleanse your mind and help you get a connection with nature. A senior is just a name that society has given older men and women over 55. But you still have many life experiences left. Being a senior does not define what you can or cannot do. Your mind and zest for life will make you feel like a young senior ready to live.

There's another form of exercise that will keep your mind and body feeling young and sharp. If you have grandchildren and you are an active part of their lives, they will always keep you feeling young. They don't know how you think or care about your age, just as long as you go to the park with them, take them to the beach or many other places, and participate in different activities with them. Children have a way of helping us to get more exercise than we want and will certainly help to keep our minds sharp with all of the questions they will ask. My grandchildren have me acting as silly as they are, sometimes chasing them outside and playing with them. My days are filled with more things to do, and I have to list everything I plan on accomplishing each day. I attribute my energy and zest for life to how I eat and the time I give to my God. I believe this is his way of blessing me in return.

CHAPTER 3

What is this Menopause Thing?

I know that estrogen is the hormone that changes a young girl's body when she is about 10 to 12 years old and starts puberty. The whole body gradually transforms from a little girl's body into a more mature young lady. She starts getting fat cells in specific body parts, such as her breasts and hips. And then, one day, you notice your little girl seems to be getting a bit shapely. A young girl will start having a monthly menstrual cycle during this time. This is so new to a young girl; she needs a mother or womanly figure to help her understand what's happening.

Estrogen will also make a young girl's voice soft and more distinguished from the male voice. Likewise, the male hormone testosterone causes the little boy to take on more manly characteristics. A little boy's voice gets deeper; the muscles and bones also grow bigger and faster than the girl's bones and muscles. Eventually, he will get hair on his face and chest area. Puberty is a part of life that most young children look forward to because most of them can't wait to be grown anyhow. Going through puberty is just a part of the cycle of life. You don't ask for it, and it's just how God made us.

In the same way, if we ladies live to our senior years, we will go through another significant change in life called menopause. I don't think too many of us are rushing to go through this change in our life. It is like puberty; we don't ask for it and cannot stop it. However, we can do some things as we age to go through them more gracefully. I look back to when I was in my early 50s, about 51 or 52 years old. I remember going to my doctor for a physical. I was doing good health-wise since I had gotten into a regular exercise regimen. I was eating healthy, considering what I used to eat: no red meats, very little sugar, and not much bread. I have always kept my weight between 140 to 147 lbs.

My blood pressure has remained steady for most of my adult years, at about 120/75, to which my doctor would reply," You must be an athlete." I chuckled and said, "No, I just try to stay active and healthy." My doctor did ask me, "Are you going through menopause yet?" I replied, "I don't know. How would I tell if I was going through menopause?" He chuckled and said, "I guess you're not because if you were, you would know." I had heard of menopause but had not talked to anyone about what would happen to me or when. My doctor informed me that I should read up on it and know what to expect because, in a few years, I would be experiencing some symptoms.

I was told my cholesterol was a bit high, and he told me some things I could do naturally to bring my numbers down. He said to limit overeating pastry and foods like cheese, bread, and red meats. He said to monitor my diet, exercise, and drink plenty of water. So I keep my appointments and encourage you to be vigilant with your health. I have been conscious of my health and pay special attention to my body and symptoms.

My doctor told me menopause was nothing to worry about but that I did need to be more informed on what to expect, so that's what I did. I started reading up on this change of life since it would affect me soon. I remember asking my mom about what changes she had gone through during her menopausal years. She replied, "I don't think I ever went through any changes in my life." My mom had been going through various health issues in her life for a few years, and amid those health challenges, she also had menopausal symptoms that she was unaware of. She said that having a hysterectomy may have affected her hormone balance. This surgery could have caused many of her other problems, but some doctors she went to during her sickness may not have thought it was menopause because she was still a relatively young woman. Later on, talking to my grandma and other family members, I thought when you sweat all the time, even when it's not hot, that you're going through a change of life, and it is wise to keep a fan with you to cool off. That's all I knew about menopause from my grandma. However, I found out this was not a sufficient remedy. Constant fanning and sweating are only two of the first symptoms of early menopause.

My mom didn't realize she was significantly deficient in the female hormone estrogen and losing bone mass and other vital nutrients to help sustain a healthy lifestyle. My mom was unaware that the many changes in her body were directly related to menopause. Just going through and studying more in-depth about this issue, I have learned so much, and if my mom had been better informed and knew more, she may not have suffered as much as a young woman. My advice is that while we are going through menopause, we should study it and build up our bodies with proper nutrients and diet. And we can avoid a lot of senior diseases.

Once a woman goes through menopause, it will interrupt her monthly menstrual cycle until it finally stops. However, it may stop for two or three months and then start back again during these months. So if a woman is fertile and still sexually active, she could have an unexpected pregnancy. It often happens when women believe they are no longer producing eggs and get slack in using birth control, resulting in a new baby in those golden years. I recall a conversation with one of my coworkers when I would see her constantly fanning herself, even in the wintertime. I asked her why she was fanning when it was cold outside. She replied, "Because I have a personal furnace burning inside me." She was about ten years older than me and later said, " Oh baby, you live on, and you will see for yourself."

I became very interested in her health because she said the same thing my doctors had said a few months earlier. I wanted to know firsthand what I could do to help myself transition more smoothly into this life change. She told me she had been going to her doctor every month because this was too much to bear. Her doctor finally put her on a hormonal patch to help build her estrogen levels. She said it helped a little, but it was worse at night. She could never get a good night's rest. She would keep the fan on her even in the winter months. She frequently opened the window to cool off when it was cold outside. This was nothing I was looking forward to; It didn't sound inviting at all. I realize hot flashes make you look like a little old lady. They are slowly diminishing your body's fluid levels, causing decreased energy levels and joint pains, and reducing your cartilage and joint lubrication. In addition, untreated menopausal symptoms can cause excess belly fat and curvature in the spine because of insufficient calcium, magnesium, and other vital nutrients.

As you age and your joints feel stiffer, you will walk at a much slower pace because those joints don't move like they used to because the synovial fluid has diminished between the joints. Losing bone mass will cause you to become the incredible shrinking woman or shrinking man in stature. It's time to get some wisdom and fight back. Do not let the doctors put you on a lot of medication if you can get a grip on your health before it becomes diseased. If you are more in tune with your body and aware of what's going on while you are relatively young, in your forties, for instance, it's time to counterbalance the changes that will affect your life as you age. Just as puberty comes and changes your life, so will menopause. It will change you from a young, vibrant woman into a slowly aging senior.

I asked my grandmother once if she was ever a young girl. She seemed always so big and old and bent over that I didn't see how she could ever have been a young girl. She replied, "Of course I was. Just live on. You never know how life, sickness, and all will change you." And that is so true, but I think that a lot of parents and grandparents didn't think of menopause as something they needed to talk about because they knew little about what to expect. Life is about living and learning. As wisdom has increased, younger women are better informed about their bodies. My grandma was 97 and walked on a cane for about 20 years. I'm glad she had the cane. It helped her to get around reasonably well. I told myself that menopause is definitely a change in your life, but you don't have to sit by and let it take over your life. I say, gird up your mind and get ready to fight back. Because there are so many things you can do that will help you gracefully age if you make some changes.

First, get on a good vitamin regimen to help build your body back up and keep it there. Next, you'll have to change your diet because some foods cause you to age faster and hold stubborn body fat, such as meats and sugar, which many people don't want to give up and often overindulge in. Next, always exercise, even if it is only lifting weights. You know how much weight is comfortable for you, then do it at least three times a week. Finally, keep those legs moving, get out, and get in a long walk, two to three times a week. Ensure you always walk in the open fresh air as much as possible. If you are going to keep a good quality of life, you cannot live a sedentary lifestyle.

You may tell yourself I don't have any energy, my knees and legs hurt too much, and I can't pull myself together. Well, this is what I'm saying to you. If you want to press past these symptoms, you cannot give in to every ache and every pain. I know it's rough. I feel the pain in my legs and hips daily, but I will not allow myself to become complacent. It is never too late. In your mind, you must continue to tell yourself I want a better life and a quality of life. I am reminded of a dear friend that lived to be 95 years old and aged gracefully. She always told me she started taking vitamins in her early forties and never overindulged in too much food. She said she decided not to do what everyone else did, like overeating and sitting around gaining weight. She said she saw so many of her family members that always ate like it was their last meal, so that made her make it a habit not to do heavy eating after 6 or 7 p.m.

This knowledge profoundly affected me because I had observed her for years. She was very vibrant, well-sized in her body, and always kept a sound mind until the end. She never walked slowly or on a cane. She could go up and down steps better than women much younger than she was. She was a wonder to behold. She said she told herself early on in life that she wanted to serve the Lord and have a good quality of life, not a life of just existing.

I have made a conscious decision that I want to do more than live. But even though I am a senior, I can still do and get around with a reasonable amount of health. I remember studying nutrition early on in college, which significantly impacted my life. I recall dissecting the ingredients in just one food, hot dogs, during that class. I will never forget seeing one ingredient in hot dogs was red erythorbate, which is red worms. So, as much as I liked hotdogs, I stopped eating them after that awakening. That's why it's easy for me to change things that are not good for my body. As I continue to study, I've learned that what we do or eat has a lasting effect on our life. Most of our eating habits are based on our upbringing as a child. Once we take control of our bodies and actions, we can create change in our lifestyle and health. Menopause is not scary. It's just a way of life, and thank God if you live to make those older years. By God's grace, you will have wisdom on what to do and how to do it better if you heed that wisdom.

CHAPTER 4

Sleepless Nights

I woke up in the middle of the night looking all around the room, and then I glanced over to see my husband still sleeping. I felt like someone had poured a glass of water all over my head and back. While collecting my thoughts, I wondered what kind of relaxation was this. Sure, I had gone through the flashes, the feeling of sweating all over my neck and face, but this was another surprise, gotcha moment. My nightgown was wet. My hair was wet, and I was exhausted. I was still working and never seemed to get enough sleep to pull a long day at work and come home to a multiplicity of things to do around the house. I can remember how some days seemed more tedious than others, especially after a day of snacking and a light work lunch. I had a good appetite, so I first wanted to prepare a delicious full-course dinner when I came home again. I prepared glazed salmon, brown rice, and smothered cabbage with carrots as a healthy eater. Now that's a meal to help settle my mind and relax my body. I always prepare something light and healthy at least three times a week. Sometimes it will help to keep my hormones balanced and better.

After a good meal and some evening news, I like to tend to the beautiful perennial flowers in my garden while I still have a reasonable amount of sunshine. Working in my garden in the evening is relaxing and brings me much solitude. It's as if I can hear my flowers saying how happy they are that I'm out there, saying "water, water, water," and telling me what they need. I also could see a fairly large amount of weeds continually forming around them, so I pulled them up from around them. Just before I water them and soak the flowers with water, I see and hear their gratitude for being so well tended to. After this, I return to the house and read a chapter in my book before getting into my comfortable bed, and hopefully, I'll get a good night's rest. I have done everything I could do to use up my little energy, and now I am tired and ready for some relaxing sleep. I'm tired, and after some tossing and turning, I finally fall asleep, only to be awakened a couple of hours later. I put my earplugs in, so I won't disturb my husband and turn on some raindrop sounds from YouTube to help me relax and hopefully fall back to sleep.

Unfortunately, sleep was hiding from me. I was tired and Restless, staring at the street light glaring through my window shade. I tried counting sheep jumping over a fence in my mind but to no avail. Sleep was still hiding. I kicked the covers off my legs. I turned from side to side, and at that moment, my husband reached his hand over while rubbing my back. He then asked, are you sick? I answered, No, I am not. He then asked why my back and gown were so wet. I said this is my new body. It's making internal changes that I cannot ignore. This was the beginning of many sleepless nights. Then I told myself, I know there has to be a natural remedy to help me out.

I wish someone would have better prepared me for what I could have done beforehand. Most of what I learned about menopause was while I was going through it, and I was in my late 50s. This brings me back to when my coworker Olivia would talk about her hot flashes. I remember her telling me she always slept under a fan, even in winter. I told myself, "Oh, I will not go through all that because everyone is different and does not go through what someone else may have gone through." Well, I can say part of that is true; don't wait until you are in a crisis before deciding what you do. I took her advice and started taking more vitamins. I never got to where I needed a patch, but if you get good advice from someone you can trust, start making a change before you get into the situation. Be wise, gather your medical information, and work on any health issues you may have right now. I didn't know the different body issues I would encounter until I was in the midst of another episode of "What's New."

I remember my husband would jump up in the middle of the night talking about his bad leg cramps and how he had to walk it out. He would moan and groan and talk about the pain, and after about five minutes, he would lie back down and say, wow, that was rough. I always thought he was exaggerating; I would say, oh, it's not that bad; you are such a drama king. I was not compassionate about his issue. You can't understand what another person may go through or his struggles until you have to walk a mile in those same shoes. I can vividly remember about a year later when, in the middle of the night, I was trying to turn over to my side, stretching and twisting, when I got a severe leg cramp. I screamed out loud.

Oh my gosh, my leg and foot were cramping and knotting up so much. I tossed and turned, trying to help it go away, but to no avail. I finally had to get up and try to walk it out. I even got some massage cream to massage it out, and it finally relaxed and went away. I could lie down for a few more hours, and the cramps returned. I wanted to cry. I have never had so many things creep in to disturb my sleep in the middle of the night. My husband looked at me and asked why you are such a big baby about it. You told me my leg cramps weren't that bad. I had to apologize. I told him, I'm sorry for taking your leg cramps so lightly because I was acting like a crybaby. The cramps just kept knotting up till I finally had to get on up.

The following day, I went to Google and looked up the cause of leg cramps. I found out that, to my surprise, I was low in potassium and magnesium and possibly needed more water. These leg cramps were a red-light warning sign, letting me know my body needed some maintenance. When your car gets low on gasoline and oil, an indicator light will tell you it's time to service or replenish your fluids. Well, the body reacts in the same way. This incredible human machine needed to be higher in magnesium levels or more daily water intake. These are just a few of the reasons you may experience leg or foot cramps; however, I found out that my magnesium levels were deficient because I had ruled out any other causes of why I started having leg cramps in the middle of the night. I had run out of liquid calcium and magnesium supplements and had taken none for about two months.

Those leg cramps were awakening me to what my body needed. I needed my nutrition built back up again. I've tried to analyze why things are happening in my body before I run to the doctor for every little ache and pain. Those leg cramps went on for about a week, and once my body could build its nutritional levels back up, I have had none recently. I always like to take liquid calcium or vitamins because they'll get into my bloodstream faster. I have always drunk 2-5 bottles of water every day, so I know it was not a water deficiency. I also increased my intake of bananas because they are fortified with lots of potassium.

I like to eat my bowl of nuts and raisin bran with strawberries and bananas on top of it for my breakfast cereal, and I've also started eating a banana as a snack before I go to bed. Sometimes I feel like a monkey for eating my bananas, but if that will help my body as far as potassium is concerned, I will eat more. However, a person with diabetes cannot eat many bananas because of the sugar content, so moderate your diet. Because my estrogen levels have dropped quite a bit, I have to do all I can to counteract the many changes that are going on in my body. As a younger woman, I could get many nutrients from my daily diet, but as I aged, I now needed more supplements to assist my slowly aging body. So often, we neglect the natural foods that are so plentiful in the supermarket and so healthy for us, such as bananas, apples, mangoes, peaches, nuts, and all sorts of green vegetables. Be moderate with the pastries. Sugary and processed comfort foods make the mouth and stomach feel so good, but they set us up for disease in the long run.

These fruits and nuts are excellent sources of magnesium and potassium. When I was younger, I had neglected so many of these great bodybuilding foods and got addicted to this American diet of processed foods, but not anymore. A good leafy salad every day, green leafy vegetables such as spinach, kale, broccoli, collard greens, and brussel sprouts will do a body good. As I age, I look for foods that will make my body heal and feel better instead of what tastes so yummy, like all those breads and desserts, big cheesy sandwiches, and more. I am happy that I retired red meats from my diet, even pork. I am not saying I don't eat any bad foods because I do. However, I know that when I eat them, it is seldom, and it is a treat I know how to eat in moderation, not just being a glutton about it.

CHAPTER 5

Diet Is Everything

Have you ever heard the old saying, you are what you eat? Well, it is true. However, it took me a few life experiences to fully comprehend this old wise saying. I can remember going on a family outing once. I think it was a Fourth of July celebration at the park. My family believed in bringing lots of food and many different variations. It is not like your typical holiday picnic; it is more like a Thanksgiving feast.

The menu for the meats was burgers, hot dogs, ribs, chicken, kielbasa, steaks, and meatballs. That was a lot of meat. The side dishes included potato salad, green beans, spaghetti, coleslaw, baked beans, and various casseroles. Oh, and don't forget a big, tossed salad, which was needed after all this heavy food. And the grand finale was the desserts. We always had cookies, cakes, banana pudding, peach cobbler, fruit salad, and cheesecake. You might say that's quite a menu for a picnic, But I warned you upfront that this was not your typical picnic. And can you imagine how a person with no self-control would act upon seeing this amount of food as if they were in a candy factory? I saw some people who started eating early during the day continue to do so throughout the day. Plus, they took a couple of plates home with them. I have learned that the human body has a separate mind of its own when feeding it. The more you provide your body, the more it craves the foods it likes until you build up an appetite for certain foods, whether good for you or not.

Your body starts saying feed me, even when you're not hungry or want to eat. Your stomach will start growling, and it will get loud on you, just like a defiant child. That's because you have never taken control of your appetite. I can say this because my body is just like anyone else's. When I say that I won't eat until a specific time, my stomach starts pouting and telling me to feed myself. But I say I'm the master over this body, and I say when it will get a meal or what it will get. I talked to my body just like I was talking to another person and discovered that it would conform.

I remember being at work one day, and it was about lunchtime; I was assisting a customer, and my stomach started growling very loud. I ignored it. Then it got louder until my customer said we better hurry up, I can see it's lunchtime. I told my stomach to be quiet, or I won't feed you today. My stomach knew I was serious, and it did not growl anymore that day. My customer said wow, do you think that will work for me. I said, "Yes, it will." I have always said I'm the captain over this body and will feed it when I want to, not when my stomach throws a tantrum like a child. This is a technique that many of you should practice, and it will help your weight and some of your medical problems.

Now back to this picnic, there was so much good food, and I overdid it that day. I had ribs, chicken, and kielbasa with coleslaw on it. My sides were macaroni and cheese, baked beans, green beans, and a salad. I knew I needed that healthy salad, so I threw it in. Isn't that what many people say, "Oh, let me add something healthy." I must say all of the food was delicious. I told myself I don't eat this much normally and would enjoy it today. Besides that, there were plenty of activities, and I participated in many of them: volleyball, badminton, and a hula hoop contest. However, once I saw everyone at the dessert table, and they had some of my favorite desserts, I eased myself over in that direction.

I got a plate and put a spoonful of peach cobbler, a little banana pudding, and a brownie. I could feel my stomach smiling and saying with every mouthful, "I like that!" I knew my stomach liked everything, but I did not want it to think this would be the norm. There was a lot of celebration, relaxation, and overeating that day, and that's okay on a special occasion. However, when this kind of eating is done far too often until it affects our health, it can be dangerous. As we get older, we need to put the brakes on. The next day I woke up feeling so stiff that my knees had a couple of big swollen spots, and my fingers looked like little swollen sausages. I got up, walking all stiff and in pain. I thought to myself, what could I have eaten that made me feel like this? I took responsibility for the feeling. I do not normally eat much soul food and I did overindulge at the picnic.

I made an appointment to see my natural health doctor. He took some blood and urine samples and analyzed them while I was at the office. He asked me what I had eaten in the last few days. I told him about our picnic and all I had eaten that day. I had gone to him several times before after I had my accident, and it was then that he had mentioned how I should avoid certain foods as much as possible. He informed me that many white blood cells were in my bloodstream, trying to eat up all the fat deposits from some of the foods I had digested. He said my body was not breaking down my fat cells as it should. Instead, it was storing them in my joints, which is why I was swollen. I knew that with arthritis, you should be careful of what and how much you eat certain foods.

I was told that different medical conditions could occur as you age since your body does not process foods like when you were younger. My doctor proceeded to mention foods I needed to eat more of and others that I should put some limits on to help cleanse my blood of all the fatty deposits and feel better. He put me on some bitter herbs and teas and then told me some foods I should eliminate from my diet, such as red meats, some cheeses, and dairy products. And above all, he told me I should limit my sugar intake; it is awful for arthritis. I said, " Well, those are all the foods I love, and I just can't do that. I loved my root beer floats, Pepsi, and other desserts. I just love them. I even like baking and cooking desserts and pies to have them around the house. I would tell myself this just in case we had company drop by. But I was the company; my husband and I were the ones eating those sweets.

This kind of thinking was before I had gone through any menopause symptoms. My doctor said then you have a decision to make. Do you want to eat everything that looks and tastes good, or do you want to feel better? I realized that with his help, I could eat many other delicious foods, and my body would appreciate it better without feeling sick after eating them.

Sugar is such an addictive food, and it should be used sparingly, which most of us can't do, especially as we age. So there we go with that age again, but it's true. We all know sweet things and delicious desserts just put a smile on our faces, but it does not put a smile on our bodies or joints. There's nothing wrong with having a good piece of cake or other desserts, but I have learned I have to put some limits on it and only do it once or twice a month.

I used to work with an older man who had a bad case of gout, and every time he went out and celebrated with his friends, he would eat some of his favorite foods and overdo it until he could barely walk and had to walk on a cane sometimes. One day after one party weekend, I saw him and asked what had happened to him. He was hopping pretty severely. "Oh, it's nothing much. I just had a great weekend, too much partying. He knew that certain foods caused him to swell up in his ankles from his gout, but here it is. He then said, "It's okay. I'll be okay in a few days." He boasted that if he drank cherry extract, it would help the swelling go down faster.

I don't understand this kind of reasoning. It's not normal behavior, and he said when he's having a good time, it does not matter. This is what I mean when I say mind-over-matter. He doesn't mind the pain as long as he is enjoying what he is doing at the time, and he'll deal with the consequences later. As for me, I choose health and wellness all the time. All I can do to help my body feel better as I age is what I will do. We are so used to this American diet and all its processed foods. Most of our prepared foods contain fats, fillers, and sugars. These foods have become such a part of our daily diet that when we eat healthy foods that don't have these ingredients, they don't taste good. As a result of our unhealthy lifestyles, there's an epidemic of high blood pressure and diabetes in our culture.

These are two major health problems that people do not take seriously, but both can be controlled with a proper diet. Unfortunately, some prefer to take as much medication as needed to continue to live an unhealthy lifestyle. My body does not process and utilize food like before I started going through menopause. I understood I needed to make some changes. I tell myself you need to drink more water, maybe a soda only on special occasions, and more tea. I have limited myself to 1 cup of coffee per week. I've increased my green tea because I've learned caffeine is not good for my body. It helps stir up my hot flashes.

All I can do to help myself is what I plan on doing, even if I must eliminate some of the drinks I love so much. I want better health. And trust me, I get it. Who doesn't love a nice warm hot piece of bread straight out the over, a big juicy sandwich, a runny grilled cheese delight, or lots of tasty pizza? I know I do, as these are my favorites. However, I know that bread turns into sugar once it hits my bloodstream. I am not a diabetic and do not plan on becoming one. I do know that the bread that I love so much is terrible for my waistline. It causes me to have a little pot belly and stirs up arthritis in my joints. I have limited the amount of bread I will eat in one week. I try to keep it down to 2 pieces per week. Some may say, "Oh no, I just can't do that. I can't let go of everything good to me. I love some warm fresh buttery bread. I'm not saying eliminate everything, but you must reduce your intake. Once you learn how to eat healthily, it will help you drop pounds, look younger and feel better.

I have learned how to make a sandwich from flatbread, and there are so many kinds: tomato flatbread, spinach flatbread, and plain flatbread. Flatbread doesn't have yeast, which is better for your body than other bread types. Just think about everything you're going through in your body and what you can do to feel better. I know that the human body was designed to rebuild itself, and that is what I continually tell myself if only I can take the time and knowledge to help myself. However, I also know that God gave us plenty of natural foods and sweeteners other than sugar to support this incredible human machine to thrive. Unfortunately, your taste buds have built up an addiction to certain foods and cravings; sometimes, those cravings can get intense. Usually, for many of us with sedentary lifestyles, we get so complacent and bored that we allow our main past-time activity to become food.

You can reprogram your body and mind to have a healthier lifestyle and to change your taste buds so that they will learn to crave foods that are good for them. But this only happens when you get sick and tired of being restricted and unhappy in your body. Food manufacturers in the industry are all about building their wealth and not your health. Some food manufacturers will put flavor enhancers, fats, and many different kinds of sugar into foods, all while knowing they are unsuitable for human consumption. They are not health providers but entrepreneurs trying to make a living. It is up to you, the consumer, to be aware of certain foods and ingredients you know would be hazardous to your health. Remember that your body parts do not function in your senior years as they did when you were younger.

Let's look at diabetes, especially Type 2 diabetes. Doctors have already told you that your pancreas is not producing enough insulin to consume all the sugar your body consumes. So your doctor puts you on a pill or insulin and tells you certain foods that will help your condition to improve, but you think that because you are given medication, you are free to continue eating everything your stomach craves and desires. Well, I have learned through the many diabetics in my family that if you don't change your diet and stop consuming so much bread, pops, and sugar, the body will slowly continue to break down until you start losing body parts or have a heart attack.

Diabetes is known to mess with the kidneys, your eyesight, and many other problems that can be avoided if you're just willing to substitute certain foods for a healthier lifestyle. In any condition, change always starts in the mind, not with another pill. We are all creatures of habit, never willing to change the old for the new. As for me, I don't want to be someone who has to constantly feel bad, aching, walking on my cane, or unable to get around well, all because I do not want to change what I do or put in my mouth. I can only talk like this because I have been the one that walked on a cane and couldn't stand up without that cane until I made up my mind that if all I had to eat was soup and broth and vegetables and fruits, that's what I was going to do. After that, I made some drastic changes. I have recreated my blood. I don't have half as many aches and pain as I used to have. I don't use the cane anymore and have a much healthier lifestyle. I know my diet made all the difference. I will tell you some of the healthy drinks I use to help with the inflammation in my body.

My Carrot Juice Drink. I used six medium-sized carrots, three stalks of celery, three to four cloves of garlic, about five inches of fresh ginger root, and one tart apple. I dice up all of my vegetables, put them in a juicer, and do this mixture up to two to three times weekly. It helps with inflammation and pain in the body. Try it. It's for anybody that wants to feel better,

My Apple Cider Vinegar Tonic. Take **one** tablespoon of vinegar into 8 oz. of warm water and one tablespoon of honey. I drink this mixture at night before I go to bed twice a week. It does wonders for the body and helps with leg cramps.

I also eat at least two to three avocados per week. I'll slice them up, put them on my salad or use them as a spread on crackers. I also make guacamole dip with them and get out my best nacho chips to use them on. So I eat plenty of salads and drink plenty of water daily, and my body says thank you, something I haven't always done.

Many different teas will help to do a body good. Try them. You have green teas high in antioxidants and ginger teas, which are good for aches and pain. Lemon teas are great for digestive problems, and don't forget chamomile or sleepy time tea, which is excellent for relaxing the body if taken about an hour before bedtime. There are many more to experiment with that help the body.

CHAPTER 6

My Eye Health

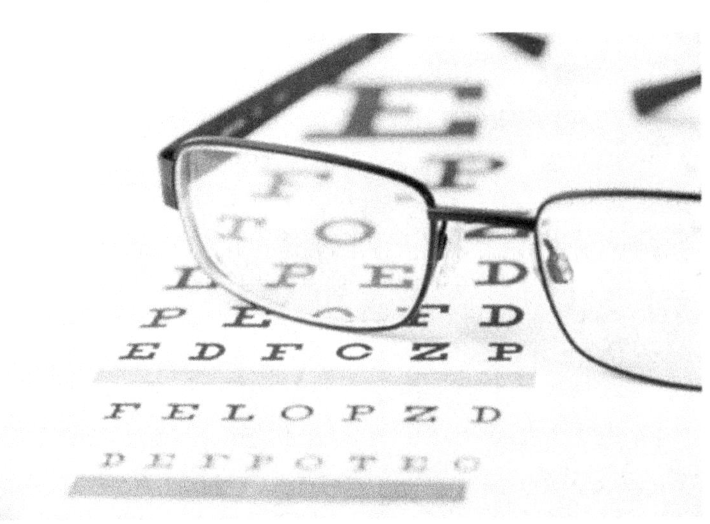

Our eyes are the windows into which we view the world. As a young lady, I did not think I needed to do too much eye care, no more than a periodical eye exam. I had been wearing corrective eyeglasses since I was in the second grade. I only needed my glasses when I was trying to see the blackboard or maybe at a far distance. My doctor told me that I had an eye problem that was called nearsightedness. I could see well enough to read without any glasses close up. However, I put on my glasses when I wanted to see writing from a distance.

As I became older, I had to get new glasses a few different times, and to my surprise, each time afterward, I was just fine with my sight again. As an adult tired of wearing glasses, I decided to switch over and get a different look, so I started wearing contact lenses. I have worn contacts for over 30 years. I could now do more to accentuate the beauty of my eyes and not let them be hidden behind a pair of glasses, or so I thought. I did not have to worry about leaving a cold room and walking into a warm room, and have my glasses fog up, or of having raindrops all over my lenses.

My contacts gave me a new sense of freedom. I could now wear eye makeup, which would not be hidden behind a pair of glasses. However, I can recall that during one of my eye doctor visits, I mentioned to my doctor how I noticed that my right eyelid seemed to be a bit droopy. Upon further examination, my doctor informed me that sometimes after wearing hard contact lenses for many years and having to pull the side of your eyes to pop them out, this could cause the eyelids to drop down a bit. However, I was told it was nothing to worry about because he could schedule a minor in-office surgery to fix the problem.

I was informed that my eye doctor could give me a numbing shot in my eyelid and do a small stitch under it to pull it back up. I wasn't sure it was nothing to worry about because he said he often does it to older patients. He said I would have to wear a patch over my eye for several days afterward; then, I should be fine. I asked him if I continued wearing my contact lenses would the condition reoccur? He informed me that as we age, our skin tends to get thinner, and there is a possibility that it could recur. But he reassured me it could always be fixed. I made up my mind after that episode that it was time for me to rethink wearing my contact lenses any longer. About a year later, I decided I didn't mind wearing glasses again.

The eyewear makers were creating some very chic eyewear. I told myself that any surgery - minor, in the office, or big - if I could avoid it, I was.

As I age, I realize how vital estrogen is even in your eye health. I noticed that my skin was not as subtle and viable as it once was. The skin on my neck and face seemed looser, and now I could see how my eyes seemed to have little bags under them. The hormone estrogen can affect the level of hormones going through the eye and cause several problems you may never have encountered before. Because of the loose skin around my eyes and on my face, I was a bit worried about the subtle changes that were taking place. I found myself standing in the mirror in the morning, trying to rub my skin back in place, just like so many other women.

I started buying all kinds of eye and facial creams to retain my original skin elasticity. Like one songwriter said, "Looking in the mirror wondering will my beauty last." I can say with certainty that our beauty will be altered if we live long enough. However, every day can bring us a new experience in our body that we don't foresee coming. I remember lying in bed early one morning, even before the sun rose when I felt a sharp stabbing pain in my eye.

I slowly opened my eyes, but the pain was still burning my eyes. I was afraid to rub them because I didn't know if I would do more harm. I got up while slowly blinking my eyes open and shut, and I went into the bathroom, got a cold washcloth, and put it over my eyes, which gave me some relief after about 10 minutes; then they started to feel normal again. I thought to myself, wondering what I did or what brought that on. My eyes were okay for about two days, then the same thing occurred again. It was just like deja vu. I got a washcloth, soaked it in cold water, and put it on my eyes. After a few moments again, I was okay. Only this time, I told my husband what had happened, and he asked me if I was okay. I told him I felt okay for now, and he said because it's happened more than once, you need to go and get it checked out, to which I strongly agreed.

I didn't know what this could be. At first, I thought maybe I had a tumor, a degenerative eye muscle, or something else in my head that could be wrong. Later that morning, I called my ophthalmologist and told him what I had been experiencing. He was able to give me an appointment for the next day. I was a bit nervous going in to see the eye doctor because I didn't know what to expect. I have heard such horror stories about people's eyes giving them problems and the doctor finding out they have brain tumors, so I was fearful. The exam took about two hours. First, he had to dilate my pupils to assess what was happening in and behind my eyes.

After my exam, my doctor informed me that the vessels and the nerves behind my eyes all looked normal. I said, thank God for that. However, he said that I had extremely dry eyes because he could see that I did not have lubrication in my eyes as I should. He said that when my eyes are closed all night, and the lubrication gets dry, that's my warning sign that something is wrong, and that's what was causing the pain in my eyes.

He also informed me that because I was going through menopause, it was the main culprit that was causing my dry eyes. He put three drops in each eye and gave me a bottle of eye drops. He told me to get a good bottle of eye drops like *Genteel* or *Refresh*. I was told to use three drops in each eye every night before bed to keep them from drying out while I slept. My doctor also said putting drops in my eyes in the morning would be wise. I have followed this regimen and have not had this eye pain anymore. However, I was informed then that my eyes were in the early stages of cataracts, and I would probably need to get them removed in a few years.

As I left his office, I said, "Wow, just another senior surprise of what can go wrong as I age." I now keep a small bottle of eye drops on my nightstand and an extra bottle in my purse. As my eyes seem to be changing, my doctor recommended getting bifocal glasses to help me see distance and read close up. I tried on a trial pair in the office, but they seemed too much to adjust to, so I opted out of the bifocals.

As I left his office that day, I was extremely grateful that my eyes were not worse than I thought. I have always heard and now know that carrots are a good source of vitamin A and beta carotene which helps to strengthen your eye health. Vitamin C tablets also help in preventing cataracts. All your green leafy vegetables are approved to be beneficial and healthy. So you see, I don't have a problem eating healthy if it means better health in any part of my aging body. It would do us all good if we got back to eating more God-given foods such as squash, kale, spinach, green beans, and more.

Eating to live should be our motto as we get older because our bodies are not what they used to be as we age. A couple of vitamins that will help maintain our eye health, such as lutein, zinc, and vitamin A. Let us do all we can to keep these windows into the world clear. We need to be able to read, drive, cook, feed ourselves, and many more things we enjoy doing. I see that each passing year brings on a new challenge. I want this body to function well with all my body parts and have a quality of life, so I'm doing everything I know how to do. If it means changing anything from how I used to do things, I will do it. By God's grace, I hope he will always give me the wisdom to desire to be a better me.

CHAPTER 7

My Two Least Favorite Places To Go

As children, we all look forward to going to pleasant places. Places like the amusement park, visiting family members, going out to dinner, going to church on Sundays, and going to the beach, make us feel good. Things not always part of our everyday routine help us light up and feel good about our day-to-day activities.

Dental Exams

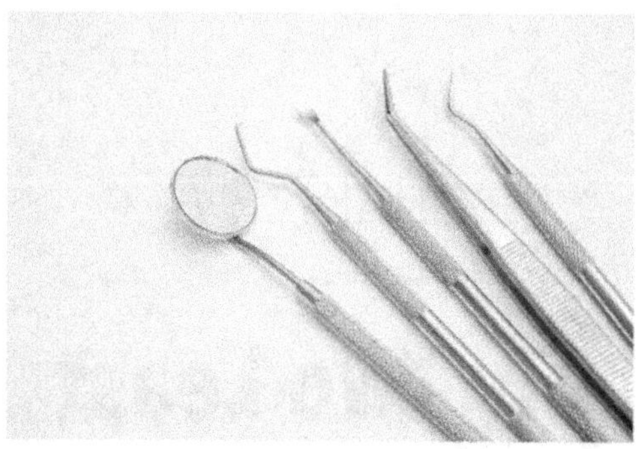

Ooh wee, what can I say? One of my least favorite places to go is the dentist. I have a fear of that place. As a young girl and adult, I've had much dental work done on my mouth. I know what it means to have needles stuck in your gums, especially as a child. Some people are so afraid of the dentist that they refuse to go, except when a tooth bothers them so much that it must be pulled. I am not at that point yet; I continually try to maintain my oral health. You see, I grew up in a large family, and we came up poor. We did not always get the necessary dental or medical care that we needed. We had a wonderful mom who gave us the best loving care she could. And my dad, well, he didn't do everything that he could have. Growing up in the 1950s and 1960s was hard for families migrating from the South to up North. Most had only the bare necessities as they came looking for better job opportunities in the North.

Our family settled in Cleveland, Ohio, because several of my dad's sisters had previously migrated to what we called "the big city." I can remember having my first dental exam when I was in the fifth grade. A young dentist came to the school and examined all the children's teeth. The school sent a slip home stating that a dental office had opened and would provide free dental care for families on government assistance. I remember my first exam at Newton D. Baker Dental School. I had several cavities in my mouth, which required multiple needles to be stuck in my gums. I cried so hard. The dentist told my mom that we had soft enamel on our teeth, probably due to not getting enough vitamin D. I know that to be true now because we did not eat healthy at all; we ate many filler foods to keep from being hungry. I was eleven when I had my first two molar teeth extracted. All I could remember was going home and getting in bed and crying the rest of the day after having my teeth pulled.

Those were some of my early dental experiences, and they have not improved. When I was young, I did not care about eating healthy food. All we knew was that we had something to eat every day. We had biscuits and gravy, oatmeal or grits, and now and then, we had some eggs. Then, for dinner, we would have some hot dogs, or maybe sometimes chicken, and lots of beans and rice. I don't recall having too much milk because that was for the babies. So, as you can see, we did not have a solid bone-building diet. But we never went hungry, and our family had plenty of love.

Going back to those early days in the dentist's chair, I remember the dentist giving me shots with a long needle in my gums. That was always so painful to me. The shots may have numbed my gums and teeth when he started the drilling, but the drilling always seemed so long and noisy. It reminded me of the men on the street doing concrete and drilling work. My lips always stayed fat and numb for a few hours after I left the dentist. I went to the dentist every month until he did all my cavities. I kept going because some of my teeth hurt from the cavities. As a child, I used to suck my thumb, which caused my two front teeth to protrude out. As I got older, I admired young people with beautiful teeth.

I wanted a beautiful smile. As a young woman, I did all I could to maintain my dental health by brushing, flossing, and keeping up with my check-ups. However, when your problems stem from childhood, your dental health is more work to maintain. As a young working woman, I decided to get some cosmetic work done on my mouth. I had a couple of caps put on my teeth where some of my early cavities that had fillings fell out. I had to have a few root canals, one of the worst dental procedures ever. As a result, I became highly anxious whenever it was time for my dental appointment. I found myself hyperventilating when I got to the dentist's office. I remember once how my dentist would sing to make me laugh and tell me it would be all right. Because I was so afraid, and the dentist was compassionate, he started giving me what's called laughing gas, and it did help calm down my fears. It did not put me to sleep, but I was calm enough to get through my appointments.

After spending a fortune to maintain my oral health, I finally felt that my smile and teeth were in a lot better shape. Now all I had to do was eat healthier, brush and floss regularly, and keep my dental appointments. Now I feel better when I go to the dentist, and all I have to do is get a cleaning and x-rays, and I'm told everything looks good. Over the past few years, my oral health has been okay, with only a cavity here or there. Since becoming a senior, though, I notice that in the past few years, I have had dental problems again, an old filling either chipping or falling out, and then it's back to the dentist telling me I need another root canal. I am much older now, and my nerves are more sensitive. I thought I was over my significant dentistry hurdles, But Here I Go Again, needing another root canal. Sometimes I am so frustrated with going to the dentist that I'm tempted to have someone pull them all out.

However, I have been told by numerous family members and friends to do all I can to maintain and keep my teeth. I remember one of my cousins who had dentures, and she would rarely wear them. I once asked her why she didn't keep her teeth in her mouth. She did look so lovely with them in. She told me the dentures hurt her gums and added, "I get tired of them in my mouth, so I do what's good for me." As afraid as I am of the needles and the drilling, I am doing my best to hold on to my natural teeth. I am now in my sixties. I recently went for a dental check-up, and I was told that I had two abscesses on my root canal and some decay that was forming under one of my caps. Okay, this time, I started crying.

I asked my dentist how this could happen, telling him I'd been keeping up with my oral health. I was told that your gums tend to recede as you age, and food particles can get under the caps and cause other issues. So, now I need to have my caps removed to see how much decay there is and if the teeth can be saved. Well, you can see and understand some of my fears that I continually hold on to as I go for my dental check-ups. When I was young, I had dental problems that I could deal with, but now I can say I'm doing all I can to see the best in every situation. I am reminded of a question I asked my grandmother once. I would see her take her teeth out of her mouth every night and put them in a container on her nightstand. "Grandma," I asked, "why do most older people get all their teeth pulled out?" She replied, "Well, they just seem to get loose and weak and give you so many problems that you just get them all pulled out." I told her I hoped I would not ever have to do that. She laughed and said, "Baby, I hope you don't either."

I can remember my dad always having a beautiful smile. His teeth looked good to me, but people don't always discuss their dental hygiene with everyone. I know that over the years, he had to have a couple of his molar teeth removed. I do remember one day going over to visit my parents. They were both in their mid-sixties, and my dad smiled at me. I noticed that he had a bare mouth. "Oh my gosh," I said, "what happened to your teeth?" I understood later that he did not go to the dentist as he should have—he only went when he had a bad toothache. After removing a few bad teeth, he was later diagnosed with a gum disease called pyria, where the gums bleed a lot and cause your teeth to become weak. He was given the option of gum surgery or pulling them all out. He decided he was tired of all the problems, so he had them all removed and got dentures. As my dad got older, he didn't like putting the adhesive on his teeth, so he just put them in his mouth. He still loved to eat a lot, and when he chewed his food, it sounded like horses galloping with all the clacking together of his teeth. He didn't care about the noise and thought we were being bossy when we brought up the sound of him eating. He would chide us: "Just wait until you get older; you may lose all your teeth and do the same thing."

I intend to keep my few natural teeth. It would be best if you did not become contrary as you age nor care about how your presence affects others. This is another reason I am trying to endure my dental exams. Even though they're unpleasant, I hope I will be happier with my teeth in the long run. I am still going to the dentist for check-ups periodically, and there is always some senior age-related problem in my mouth when I go. So I have to continue to try to keep my oral health up. If I ignore the health of my teeth, I know that I'll be spending lots of money correcting difficulties and problems because of bad dental health.

Those Annoying Pelvic Exams

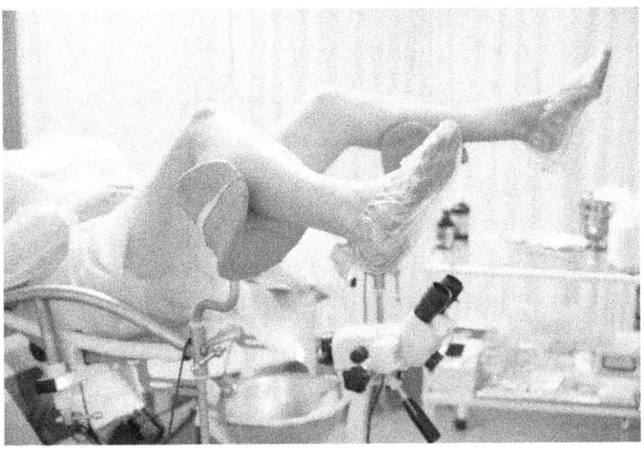

I remember that my last OB-GYN pelvic exam was pretty difficult. As I have gotten older, I find I am not as flexible as I once was. I also suffer from arthritis. As a result, these exams have become very traumatizing for me. I remember talking to my grandmother a few years back while she was still with us. I would take a vacation every year and visit her for two weeks. I once asked her if she still got pelvic exams. She was happy to fill me in: *"No baby, I don't have any reason to go get an exam between my legs. I don't have no husband, and I ain't looking for one, and I don't have any menstrual flow anymore. I ain't got no man I'm having sex with. I don't itch down there, so I ain't letting no doctor put that cold piece of metal inside of me no more."* Grandma was about seventy-five years old then and lived to be ninety-seven years. Well, I told myself, I guess I had better continue with my exams.

Even though I no longer have a menstrual cycle, I have a husband, and we are still active. So, until recently, I have never had any preconceptions about going in for my annual pelvic exam. But, since I had arthritis, and my joints and hips are not flexible like when I was younger, my last gynecological exam was a bit too much. I had to psych myself up for it.

On one of my office visits, I sat in the waiting room hyperventilating and taking deep breaths, wondering if this exam would be as difficult as my last one. Finally, when it was time to be called into the exam room, I expressed my fears and anxiety to my doctor, a young woman in her mid-thirties. She assured me it would not be as bad as I had made it out to be, but she didn't understand that when you have arthritis and other joint problems, the procedure feels different. My doctor asked me several questions: "Do you have any vaginal discharge?" I replied, "No." "How about any itching or bleeding?" I also replied "No" to that question. Then there was a big private question: "Are you still sexually active?" I answered, "Well, I still have a husband, so that's a yes." She replied, "How is that for you?" I replied, "Well, it's okay, and thankfully it's not with a cold piece of metal, and my body stretched out in discomfort." She laughed and said, "Okay, you can get on the table." I felt like a young girl when her boyfriend is trying to comfort her in her first sexual experience, telling her the experience won't hurt. My doctor proceeded with the exam, telling me to put my feet in each stirrup and slide to the table's edge with my legs wide open. "You'll be fine," she said." You are a pro at this by now."

So, I just went to the edge of the table, but the hip joints would not let me open my legs like she was trying to get them. I told my doctor this was what I was talking about. The wider I tried to move them, the more they seemed like they would pop out of the socket. Finally, she said we would try another way, which didn't work well. I felt like I was having a baby. I screamed in pain, but I guess she was tired also, and she proceeded anyway to do the exam. She said I was not her only patient today, so let's get this done. When she finally finished the exam, I wiped tears away from my eyes. I had to admit that this was now the state of my body; arthritis and joint problems making everything so much more difficult. Getting old is not for chumps, but I'll admit that there are times like this when I am a chump. Through all of my fears, panic, pain, and biopsies, I was still in one piece when the session ended. And after a bit of counseling from my doctor, I was back in a good mood before I left the office. However, on my way home, I told myself that if all was well with this exam, I didn't think I would do this again.

The experience had been a nightmare for me, an experience that I did not want to repeat. I know that many women in their 60s and 70s are in a lot better physical shape than I am. Some women do not have joint problems at all. Hurray for them. Please continue to get your annual vaginal exams. I have started more pelvic exercising and walking as much as possible to keep these muscles and joints mobile. Do all you can not to get hooked on taking so much medication. I was taking a couple of drugs over twenty years for my arthritis that helped to mask my pain, but it was destroying my joint cartilage and building up calcium deposits.

I remember asking my doctor what I could do to help lessen my joint pains and improve the mobility of my body. He suggested that it may be time to get a hip replacement. No one wants hip replacements if possible because that is a last resort. However, I am still moving reasonably well with my natural hips, and hopefully, something will give up eventually, and I'll feel better. If you can nutritionally keep a medical problem under control, have enough strength to do that. We should do all that we can to age gracefully.

I am not on any prescription medication now, but I must take *Aleve* when I have a difficult day. Finally, I have taken control of my health; my joints and legs feel much better. I had to learn the hard way through the experience, but there is always time to start helping yourself. Through the pelvic exams, I realized that my joints were getting worse. I knew I had better control my health to regain my body strength. So, here I am ten years later, finally reversing my painful joints.

I say to married or romantically inclined couples; it is up to you to keep yourself in the best physical shape you can. That goes for you men, too. I know that as men age, they all tend to have problems with their prostate gland. Many men have burned out that little gland with overuse and not maintaining regular health check-ups. I know that even if you don't have a joint mobility problem, men can cause women problems that can affect women's pelvic exams. Some men feel they do not have to bathe as often as women, and these men neglect their pelvic health. I have heard men say that women have to wash and clean every day, but men don't have to because they don't believe men carry the kind of odor that a woman does. Some men think they only have to bathe every two to three days. I'm afraid I have to disagree with that; everybody should bathe every day, especially as you become a senior.

Our vaginal health is vital when we are young women and more so when we are older women. Whether we are married or not, we should be very concerned about this body to maintain it to the highest standard of purity. I know of a single senior woman in her early 80s whose husband died about five years ago, and she made it known amongst a few of her friends that she would like a male companion. She was looking for someone who was still active and could get around on his own. One of her friend's husbands introduced her to a senior male. They had their first lunch date, and he seemed very nice and mobile; he could still drive and loved dancing.

Over the next several months, they maintained a pleasant telephone conversation. However, in one of the conversations, the older woman asked the man if he was looking for a sexual relationship. He told her he just wanted a good female friend he could take out some time, just someone to talk with and go places with. He explained to her that he was not very good sexually because of an inactive prostate gland and other male problems. Thus far, these two have maintained a great companionship because they both had been married and just wanted someone they could care for and spend their time with. As I see it here, the important thing is that they were honest with what they wanted.

Most young people would not accept a relationship like this, but age can change our mindset. Our senior population has seen a rise in pelvic diseases because many seniors feel that since they can't have babies anymore, they do not need to be as careful as they were when they were younger. A little advice to everyone reading this: single women, love yourselves. You can now have a satisfying platonic relationship with someone of the opposite sex, and you do not have to prove your womanhood or manhood to each other. Most seniors already have children and have been married before, so why not make the most of your golden years and enhance the friendships you make now by showing kindness and respect to each other? As for this older woman I was talking about earlier, she found great happiness in a new friendship with a man who was not only a great ballroom dancer but someone who loved to drive. They enjoyed many evenings out, having dinners and going to concerts together. Wow! What a great alternative to being alone!

CHAPTER 8

Osteoporosis and Osteopenia

I can reflect on a time about four years ago when I was moving like a turtle on a site-seeing mission. I was moving slower and slower as the days went by. This thing just suddenly happened over the course of about two months. My ankles were weaker than usual, and now I was experiencing pain in my groin area. I had never felt this before. I would lose my balance if I didn't watch how I suddenly turned, something I have never had a problem with before. When I have doctor appointments, I have to leave much earlier to allow myself time not to rush. I even found myself occasionally using my late mom's cane to help steady my walking. I realized that a cane is a great companion for those who need it. I can remember when my dad was about 85 years old, his walking had gotten a little wobbly, and he was always holding onto chairs or the wall as he walked around. I told him he needed a cane to steady himself as he walked. He replied that canes are for old people, and I said, "What do you think you are? You are an old man." He laughed and said, "Oh, I guess I am getting old, right?" After that, my dad started using a cane all the time.

I told him about the time my husband took me to the grocery store one Saturday morning, and I had such a hard time getting in the car, especially lifting my legs to put them inside the vehicle. I was only in my early sixties and genuinely exasperated once I got my seatbelt on. I told my husband, "Wow, this is almost too much." Then, I recalled watching a few episodes on the History Channel of ancient alien encounters later that day. I wondered if I had had an actual alien encounter while I slept. It was as if somebody had switched my good legs and replaced them with someone else's bad legs. This story was how my mind was justifying my now intense leg pain.

Okay, let's get back to the supermarket in the parking lot. A car pulled up right next to my car, and an old lady about 80-plus years old had her husband help pull her out of the vehicle. Yet, once she got out, she was still all bent over. He gave her a cane, and she slowly walked towards the door, holding onto his arm. In the meantime, my husband had also come around and helped me get my legs out of the car and stand me up. I noticed the older couple glanced over at my car. I told my husband I bet she thinks I'm mocking her because I got out of the car as she did. I could stand up straight with my cane and was about 20 years younger than her. We noticed each other in the store, and I thought, wow, I can still get worse if I don't do something to help change my condition. Well, that's when I decided to take a yoga class. It was an early morning class, at about 9:00 am. A class early enough to help stretch sufficiently to get the nighttime kinks out of my joints. I had always heard that yoga helps the whole body. Even better, it was a senior chair yoga class.

We had a class of about 25 men and women. Even though they all looked older than I was, they all seemed to be able to move better than I could, even the ones on the walkers. I stuck with the class for about two months, but it was too much for me then. Regardless of the pain and the slow walking, I always stay physically active, including travel. I continue to make visits to Georgia and, quite often, to Florida.

However, I fell a couple of times within a month. I decided I had better go in to see my doctor. I also had not been feeling up to doing my volunteer gardening that I was doing twice a week. The bending and walking had become too much for me to continue. I told my doctor my alien encounter story. My doctor reviewed my last test results and told me my previous bone density test did not look good. I had just recently started seeing a new rheumatologist because my previous doctor had retired after I had been his patient for about 15 years. He was a good doctor, and we had a good patient, doctor relationship.

He always kept up with my results and discussed my progress with me. And as far as he could see, I was in pretty good shape; he would also tell me to try and eat right for my arthritic condition, which I always tried to stick to. I remember the first time I saw my new doctor; she introduced herself and asked me how I felt. I told her I had recently been feeling a lot more pain in my ankles and felt like my groin and hip areas were paining me a little more. She said, " Well, you do have arthritis, and sometimes it can be more painful than other times. So we talked a bit more about the medication I was taking. Finally, she said, " Well, let's look at some of your last test results and see if I can see anything different. So she looked over and compared my different test results. She said, "I see what your problem is. You have osteoporosis." "How do you know? I asked. None of my doctors have ever mentioned osteoporosis to me before." She said, "Well, your dexa test scan, which is a bone density test, definitely shows a lot of bone loss."

As you probably can imagine, I was stunned to hear this. I knew nothing about this disease besides it being an older person's bone disease. I sat there for a moment to try and collect my feelings. Then, I asked her what I could do to correct it or to make my bones stronger. By this time, she was writing out a prescription for Fosamax, and sending it to my pharmacist. She told me to start on it right away, once a week, first thing in the morning, with a full glass of water while sitting straight up. Do not lie down for at least an hour after taking it. Then, wait to eat anything for at least one hour. She handed me some paperwork, left the office, and said I will see you in four months. Wow, I said this was a bit much to swallow at one time, and so she did not tell me anything else. I left the office almost in a daze.

This doctor's mannerism was rough compared to what I was used to dealing with my previous doctor. I went to the pharmacist to pick up my prescription. The pharmacist asked me if my doctor had told me how to take this medicine, and I said, "Yes, I'm aware of what to do." I am hesitant to take any medication with these kinds of precautions, so I took the caution insert and read it cover to cover. It was a bit much, especially some of the harsh side effects. Something did not sit right in my spirit about this medication, so I asked several family members if anyone had heard of this Fosamax. To my surprise, my sister-in-law asked me how did you get osteoporosis. You stay more active than all of us. That's what I was also wondering. You're always trying to tell everybody else what to do health-wise. Then she said, " I think that's the medication they put my sister on. Let me call her and check to see if that's what she was taking.

A little while later, her sister called me to tell me she had been diagnosed with osteoporosis a year earlier, and they had put her on Fosamax. She told me all the side effects she had encountered in just two months. She begged me not to take it. She said a group of women had banded together and tried to get that medication banned from the medical pharmacist. She told me she had started out having severe headaches. She tried to take an aspirin to help the headaches, and then the pain started on her face until she got lockjaw. She had to go in to see her doctor after the exam.

She was admitted immediately to the hospital. She said she had brain surgery because of Fosamax's effects on her head. She was directly taken off Fosamax and was hospitalized for about a month. She told me she still had problems with her jaw and esophagus. It was hard for her to swallow. I know medicine affects everyone differently, but after reading about the numerous women filing lawsuits and their complications, I decided not to take this medication. So, I started doing my research on how to strengthen my bones. I was already taking vitamins, but I guess I was not getting enough of the necessary nutrients I needed. So, I started ensuring I was getting at least 1200 mg of calcium and magnesium daily. I increased my vitamin D3 intake and tried to get as much natural vitamin D from sun exposure as possible. I made sure I limited my sugar intake because I've always heard how sugar can cause bone problems and decrease joint cartilage as you age. I look at the numerous seniors who seem to be suffering from joint and bone issues. I think it must be something in the water we are also drinking.

My bones and joints became so fragile that I had to start walking on a cane. I was determined to take everything I knew would help strengthen my bones and joints because I did not plan on walking on a cane for the rest of my life. By this time, I had changed my diet, continued taking the proper amount of vitamins, going to the gym, working on the leg machines, and lifting comfortable weights. I found that my leg discomfort was getting better. I have always exercised and scheduled body massages, but now I get them monthly, which helps blood circulation. I've noticed that I don't have to use my cane as much anymore. Gradually, after about nine months, I walked again without any cane and with minimal pain in my legs and groin. I attributed it to increasing my specific vitamins and having the correct dosage. You will be surprised at the many changes occurring in your body during menopause as it starts losing necessary nutrients that are not replenished. I can now walk about two miles without my cane in my neighborhood at least three days a week. I may not do everything I used to do when I was younger, like riding a bike or skating or playing tennis, but I do stay active, with some kind of continual motion

I am feeling good in my joints and legs. It is time for me to go back and meet with my rheumatologist for my follow-up to see how I'm doing. When she asked me how I was doing, I told her I'm feeling okay. She asked me how my arthritis was doing. I said it is in control. I told her I was uncomfortable with the Fosamax that she had prescribed, so I did not take it. She looked in her laptop computer at my test results, then asked me why I was taking Fosamax. I told her because you prescribed it and said I needed it for my osteoporosis. She didn't recall saying anything like that. She said I could only go by what I see on my computer. I'm looking at your dexa scores, and they do not show that you have osteoporosis.

I told her you prescribed the medication, and you told me how to take it. She said it must have been a mix-up with someone of the same name, and when it was caught, it was corrected in the computer. As you can see, I was very upset about the mix-up, and I said, what if I didn't listen to my gut instinct and had taken a strong prescription medication that I did not need? I said don't you see in your system where you prescribed Fosamax? She admitted she was glad I did not take it and that my dexa scores showed that I had osteopenia and was taking the right vitamins to help strengthen my bones. I did not push the prescription issue further because I did not take the medication. Still, I would have been highly distraught to think that I was taking that kind of medication and never needed it, especially with the many potential side effects that could have occurred. I understand that computers and humans are all subject to error, and I'm just thankful that the Angels were leading and guiding me in this situation.

My doctor took the mix-up so lightly and said she was glad the system corrected the mistake. I am so happy I relied on natural cures than on some doctor quickly writing out of prescription. I want my bones and joints to remain in optimal shape so that I can do everything I have planned for my golden years. See, I want to be an example to prove to others that you do not have to accept every medical issue that tries to overtake your body, even if the doctor says it is. I am very aware of any changes in my health because I self-evaluate what's going on with my legs, back, and other body parts every week. I know that when any changes occur, all I have to do is look back over everything I have eaten in the last couple of days, and I will find out what the culprit is. As we age, we must be conscious of certain foods that do not agree with our bodies.

I have learned that if I want to feel at my best every day, I need to eat a nutritional meal to cause my body to strengthen and eliminate any toxins I may have ingested. In addition, I recently decided to go to a chiropractor to see if my body was out of alignment because bumps, bruises, and twists and turns can cause fragile joints to miss alignment. So I started going to this chiropractor, and after about three visits, I could feel a remarkable difference in my leg pain. She told me that a tiny shift in your spine could cause discomfort, and I found that true. So I continually do all I can to stay in optimal health and pain-free.

Just because I'm getting older, I notice that doctors are continually trying to put me on more and more medication. I do not feel that I must be confined to a life of pain and sickness or medicines because I'm getting older. Instead, I do everything I have learned by changing my diet and continuing to exercise. I do many things to have an excellent quality of life. Still, no one would believe my body's condition a few years ago and the condition I'm in now. I go to the gym regularly, take walks, and have noticed that the pain in my body has decreased by 80%, and I'm looking forward to feeling better and better. I hope whoever reads this will understand that you are who you are because of what you eat and do. But that's only if you do not have some genetic condition or something you were born with. If you were once healthy, you could retain that. It is so true that as a man thinketh, so is he.

CHAPTER 9

Inner Strength

I am very grateful to God that I have lived long enough to be called a senior. When I recall how many people have been cut down in the prime of their lives or as adolescents, it makes me more diligent in caring for my total health. I have encountered many health challenges along the way and in this body, but I have never been one to accept everything that happened or was thrown at me. I am very familiar with the passage in the Bible where Paul says in Philippians 4:13, *"I can do all things through Christ, who strengthens me."* It takes strength to walk in senior shoes. It is not for the faint of heart. Jesus said in John 10:10, *"I came that you might have life and that more abundantly."* I always tell myself that sickness and pain do not equal an abundant life, so I stand on God's word and encourage myself.

Sickness and pain will rob you of your joy and strength. So each time they gave me a medical diagnosis, I was a little down in my spirit, but once I pulled myself back together, I reminded my body that this too shall pass. I felt the pain and got the results, but I could never let it get into my spirit. So, as Proverbs 23:7 says, *"As a man thinketh in his heart, SO IS HE!"* (My emphasis added)

I have had to readjust my diet frequently. I have gone on a spiritual fast to inquire about our great God in heaven, who made this body, and what I need to do to regain a reasonable portion of my health and strength. He always directs me to people, doctors, or solutions to help me. But unfortunately, many people accept everything the doctors tell them and will do nothing to help themselves. For example, let's say that your doctor told you that you needed to lose some weight and try to increase your water intake.

A person who wants a good quality of life will do all to adhere to this advice, but some people have somehow attributed certain foods to having a good time without limits. I have always proposed that I do not need to eat everything called food, and I certainly don't need an overabundance of any food. That is what you call gluttony, and when you get into the mindset that says, "I'm going to do what makes me happy," you are not considering your body nor the long-term effects it will have on your body and mind. That's when sickness sets in. The body doesn't need half of what we give it. Another scripture in the Bible says, *"For everything in the world—the lust of the flesh, the lust of the eyes, and the pride of life—comes not from the Father but from the world."* 1 John 2:16. And everything that we see in the world, we do not need it. Learn how to talk to your mind so that your body will have no choice but to conform.

Do you know why there are so many alcoholics who do not know how to resist a drink? It's because when he has an urge for a drink, he constantly feeds that urge with another drink daily. He doesn't allow himself to dry out or say no to the desire that pulls on his body. That's the same with a person with diabetes who has to take insulin continually. They never say no to any urges, even when this urge destroys the inner body.

Type 2 diabetes is controllable by diet. However, many people have said that if I can take a pill or shot and still eat everything I want, I will do that. The body, especially the pancreas, continually breaks down if you don't change your eating habits. All people with diabetes know that too many carbs are the culprit to their disease, and most of them are unwilling to use their inner strength to say no. Enough, I'm taking control of my health from now on. I continually tell myself that I am sick and tired of being sick.

If there's something that I can do to help myself feel better, I'm going to do it. My body is like a ship, and I am the ship's captain. I will not let it run off course and do what it wants to do, especially if it means a wreck. No, I don't think so. Life can be a beautiful thing. God made a beautiful world, and if we recognize our Creator, love, and treat our families and others the way we want to be treated, life will have more meaning. Don't be a lazy person. Seek wisdom even in your golden years and continue to seek education. Study something you are passionate about, whether cooking, sewing, gardening, or whatever, and keep your mind busy and active.

Above all, keep that body in motion. A body in motion stays in motion and makes for a happier lifestyle. As I see it, God has allowed me to have a long life with reasonably good health, except for a few aches and pains and many bumps along the way. But thank God, troubles and pain don't last always. He has given me a small nest egg and abundant wisdom to share with my children and grandchildren. I have surrounded myself with family and friends, for whom I am continually grateful. I realize these are blessings from the Almighty, and he has allowed me to enjoy them. I am reminded of a passage in his word that says, follow peace with all men, do not hold in your heart bitterness toward anyone. The result of bitterness is sickness and depression, and early death.

If we learn how to smile more and be kind to children, we may even find one of them that will become your hands and your feet and especially your friend. I started writing this book to help some sickly withdrawing seniors realize they can improve their quality of life with friends and family daily by changing some foods they consume. I continue to tell myself that today will be better than yesterday and use the power of words. It's very effective once you get them in your spirit. In Romans 4:17(b), the Bible says to speak those things that are not as if they were. If you want a better life or better health, speak it into your mind. Speak it until it gets in your heart. This also takes a measure of faith; we need to understand that these are just temporary bodies that we're living in, and we need to do all we can to have a quality of life while we are mobile enough to do that. Life is like running a race; do all you can to finish even if you don't come in first place.

About the Author

Deborah and granddaughter, Jayda.

Deborah is a woman of diverse talents and has worked as a medical assistant, a professional dressmaker, an accountant, and a business clerk with the U S. Postal Service, from which she retired after 38 years. She is a licensed Elder and teaches a weekly Bible study. However, nutrition and horticultural gardening have taken hold of her heart for the past twenty-five years, leading her into a part-time business developing beautiful yards. Her strong desire and love for people have motivated her to write about a few of her senior moments and life experiences to encourage others to persevere and be their best as they age. Deborah is a wife, mother of two adult children, and grandmother.

For more information or to have Deborah share how to age well, contact her at <u>wellsbaby66@gmail.com</u>.